Goldilocks

Including Beauty & The Beast & The Ugly Ducking

igloo

Goldilocks and The Three Bears

nce upon a time there was a lovely little cottage that sat right in the middle of the woods. In this cottage lived a family of friendly bears. There was Big Papa Bear, who could be a little grumpy at times, Medium-sized Mama Bear, who was just as a mother should be and Teenie Weenie Baby Bear, who liked to play all day.

One fine day they all stomped down to the kitchen for their usual breakfast of delicious homemade porridge. Papa Bear ate his porridge out of a big bowl, Mama Bear ate her porridge out of a medium-sized bowl, while Teenie Weenie Baby Bear had his very own teenie weenie bowl.

Papa Bear scooped up a large spoonful of porridge and popped it straight into his mouth. "Ouch," he cried. "That's too hot!" Mama Bear tasted hers. "Ooh, I suppose it is a bit hot," she agreed.
"It will burn my mouth!" cried Teenie Weenie Baby Bear after tasting his.

"I've got a good idea," said Mama Bear. "Why don't we go for a walk in the woods? By the time we get back, our porridge will be cool."
"Oh, all right," said Papa Bear a bit grumpily. He really would have liked to go back to bed until his porridge cooled down.
"Yippee!" yelled Teenie Weenie Baby Bear. "I can show you how fast I can run." So, shutting the door behind them, the three bears went for a walk in the woods.

Not long after they had gone, a little girl called Goldilocks, who was out walking in the woods, stumbled across the little cottage where the three bears lived. She thought it was so lovely that she wanted to look inside. She carefully opened the door and shut it quietly behind her.

The first thing she noticed were the three bowls of porridge on the kitchen table.
"They look really yummy," she thought. "I'm so hungry. I'm sure no one would mind if I ate just a little."

First, she tried a spoonful of porridge from the big bowl. But that was too salty.
Next, she tried a spoonful of porridge from the medium-sized bowl. But that was too sweet.
Finally, she tried a spoonful of porridge from the teenie weenie bowl. That was just right. Goldilocks was so hungry she ate every last bit. She felt tired after eating so much and decided to sit down for a while.

First, she tried to sit in a big chair but it was so big, her feet didn't even touch the ground.
Next, she tried a medium-sized chair. That was a little better but she could only reach the ground with her toes.
Finally, she sat in a teenie weenie chair and that was just right. But she was far too big for the teenie weenie chair and, when she sat down in it, she broke it!
"I wonder if there are any beds upstairs," she thought. "I'm sure no one would mind if I lay down for a while."

She went upstairs and saw three beds.
The first bed she tried was a big, floppy bed. "This bed is far too soft," she thought.
The next bed was a very neat, medium-sized bed. "This bed is far too hard," she thought.
Finally, she lay on a teenie weenie bed. "This bed is just right," thought Goldilocks, and was soon fast asleep.

When the three bears returned from their walk, they were very hungry and looking forward to eating their porridge. The first thing they saw were the spoons lying in the porridge bowls.

"Who's been eating my porridge?" cried Papa Bear in a big, grumpy voice.

"Who's been eating my porridge?" cried Mama Bear in a medium-sized voice.

"Who's been eating my porridge, and eaten it all up?" cried Teenie Weenie Baby Bear in a teenie weenie voice.

Papa Bear was so grumpy he decided to have a sit down, but noticed that the cushion on his chair was messed up.

"Who's been sitting in my chair?" he cried in his big, grumpy voice.

"Who's been sitting in my chair?" cried Mama Bear in her medium-sized voice, noticing that her cushion was messed up, too.

"And who's been sitting in my chair and broken it?" yelled Teenie Weenie Baby Bear in his teenie weenie voice.

"This is making me really grumpy," said Papa Bear in his big, grumpy voice. "I'm going to bed." The other bears agreed and followed him up the stairs.

When they got there, they saw that their beds had been messed up, too.

"Who's been sleeping in my bed?" cried Papa Bear in his big, grumpy voice.

"Who's been sleeping in my bed?" cried Mama Bear in her medium-sized voice.

"And who's been sleeping in my bed, and is still sleeping in my bed?" cried Teenie Weenie Baby Bear in his teenie weenie voice.

All this shouting woke Goldilocks. When she saw the three bears looking down angrily at her, she leaped out of bed, ran down the stairs, out the door and into the woods as fast as she could. And the three bears were very pleased that they never saw her, ever again.

Beauty and The Beast

L ong ago, there lived a rich merchant who had three sons and three daughters. Unfortunately, his sons were only interested in hunting and fishing, while his two eldest daughters were greedy and selfish. However his youngest daughter was liked by everyone. Everyone called her "Beauty". Not only was she very beautiful to look at, she but was the kindest person that anyone had ever met.

One day, the merchant heard some terrible news. All the ships carrying his goods had sunk at sea in a storm, which left him with hardly any money. The whole family had to move from their grand house to a little cottage. While the merchant and his sons worked hard all day in the fields, his daughters stayed at home doing the housework. The two eldest daughters were very lazy and sat around doing nothing. Beauty, however, enjoyed her work around the cottage, happy to be helping her father in these difficult times.

One morning, a letter arrived for the merchant. It said that one of his ships had not sunk and it was going to arrive at the port the following morning.
"Maybe we're not so poor, after all!" said the merchant, happily. With great excitement, he set off to meet his ship. Before he left, he asked his daughters what they would like as gifts. The eldest daughters asked for jewels and beautiful clothes but Beauty, who didn't have a greedy bone in her body, simply asked for a single red rose.

When the merchant got to the port he found out that there was no ship coming in. Later that night, there was a huge storm, and the merchant lost his way.

He saw lights in the distance. Getting closer, he realized that the lights shone from a castle. He rode up to the castle, and knocked on the door. It creaked open.

Inside, he found a roaring fire and food on the table, but only one plate. There was no one else around, so he sat down and ate. He ventured upstairs. One of the bedrooms was warm, with freshly ironed sheets laid out on the bed. "It's almost as if I was expected," thought the merchant, before climbing into bed and falling fast asleep.

When he awoke, he took a single rose from the garden for Beauty. Suddenly out of the bushes an ugly beast appeared, "You eat my food, sleep in my bed, and steal one of my roses?" The merchant told the Beast it was for his daughter Beauty. "Very well," the beast said, "You may leave if your daughter takes your place."

Sadly, the merchant agreed that he had to let Beauty go. With a heavy heart, he waved her farewell as she set out for the Beast's castle. When she got there, she found to her great surprise that the Beast was very kind to her. He showed her around the castle and its beautiful grounds and then took her to her room.

The Beast had made sure that all the books she'd like to read and all the little ornaments she'd like to look at were there. There was even a magic mirror in which she could see her family back at home. "This Beast may be ugly, but he is very considerate," thought Beauty.

On that first evening, the Beast came to eat supper with her. From then on, it was the same every evening. Beauty and the Beast would have supper together after spending long days in the library reading or walking out in the grounds.

Time passed. Then, one evening, Beauty looked into the mirror and saw that her father was very ill. She begged the Beast to allow her to go home and care for him.

"Very well," said the Beast. "But you must return here within a week. When you are ready to come back, put this ring on your dressing table at home and I shall know you want to return here. If you don't do this within one week, I shall die."

Beauty agreed, and when she woke up the next morning, she found herself in her own bed at home.

She cared for her father day and night over the next few days, and soon one week had passed. Although her father was getting better, Beauty had been so busy, she hadn't noticed how quickly the days had passed.

One night, Beauty had a dream that the Beast was lying dead by the side of the lake in his castle grounds.

"I must go back to him," she thought. She put the ring he gave her on her dressing table, and the next morning found herself back in his castle. She ran down to the lake and was horrified to see that the Beast was lying on the ground, barely alive.

"Oh, Beast," she cried, "I did not mean to stay away so long. Please come back to me. You are so good and kind." Then, she kissed him.

Suddenly, the Beast changed right in front of her eyes. All signs of his ugliness had disappeared and there was a handsome prince in his place.

"Beauty, my love," explained the Prince. "I had a spell cast on me many years ago that turned me into an ugly beast. The only way it could be broken was if a girl who loved me, kissed me in spite of my ugliness."

Beauty kissed him again and vowed that she would stay by his side forever. The happy couple rode to her father's house where they were married. Then they journeyed back to the castle where they lived in complete happiness for many years to come.

The Ugly Duckling

It was summer in the country. Everyone felt hot and lazy in the strong sun. In the moat that surrounded the old castle, a mother duck had laid her eggs among the rushes. She had sat for a long time waiting for her brood to hatch. Finally, one by one, the eggs began to crack and she heard the first "quack, quack" of her new ducklings.

Soon, all the eggs had hatched except for one. This was the largest egg of all and it was becoming very difficult for the mother duck to sit comfortably on it.

"Are you all right?" asked a friendly duck, who happened to swim by.

"I'm fine, thank you," replied the mother duck. "It's just that my last egg here is taking a long time to hatch. As you can see, it's quite big to get comfortable on, especially in this heat."

"Yes, you do look tired," said the friendly duck. "I'm sure it will hatch soon."

Just then, both ducks heard a tiny scraping sound and then a cracking sound as the egg began to break. Suddenly, out popped the last duckling. It was the strangest, ugliest-looking duckling either of them had ever seen.

"Oh, dear," said the friendly duck. "What an odd shape he is. He must have been in the shell too long."

"Never mind," said the mother duck. "I'm sure he'll look just like my other ducklings in a few weeks. Anyway, he's my son and I love him whatever he looks like."

"Of course," grinned the friendly duck and, with a "see you later!" paddled gently away.

"Come on, everyone," said the mother duck to her new ducklings. "Let's get you swimming." All the ducklings lined up behind their mother and, with their little legs paddling furiously, swam towards the middle of the moat.

"Here's mother duck with her new ducklings," all the other ducks cried, when they saw the little procession.
"But look at that one on the end," said one, pointing to the ugly duckling.
"That's the ugliest duckling I've ever seen!" said another.
It seemed that all the ducks in the moat were laughing at the ugly duckling.

As the weeks went by, the ugly duckling's brothers and sisters grew bigger and stronger. They looked more and more like proper ducks with each passing day. But the ugly duckling seemed to grow even stranger-looking, with his dull, grey feathers and peculiar shape. Because he looked different, the other young ducklings laughed at him, and didn't want him to play with them. The ugly duckling felt so sad and lonely he began to hide among the tall rushes where no one would see him.

Once, he saw three beautiful, white birds flying overhead. They seemed so happy and free. In some strange way he felt he was related to these lovely birds in the sky. "But how could I be?" he thought. "They are so beautiful and I am so ugly." And so he stayed in his hiding place among the reeds where no one would see him.

When winter came, the waters of the moat froze over and the ugly duckling was stuck fast in the ice. He couldn't move at all, not even to get food. As the days went by, the ice showed no sign of melting and it seemed that the ugly duckling might starve to death.

One day, a man passed by and noticed the poor duckling stuck in the ice. The man was kind and he brought his axe to free the duckling. Tenderly, he lifted the ugly duckling from the frozen waters and took him home.

The man cared for the ugly duckling as if he was his own child, keeping him warm and making sure he had enough to eat. But, as comfortable as life was in the man's house, the ugly duckling knew that he did not really belong there. So, when the waters of the moat thawed out, he went back to his hiding place in the reeds once more.

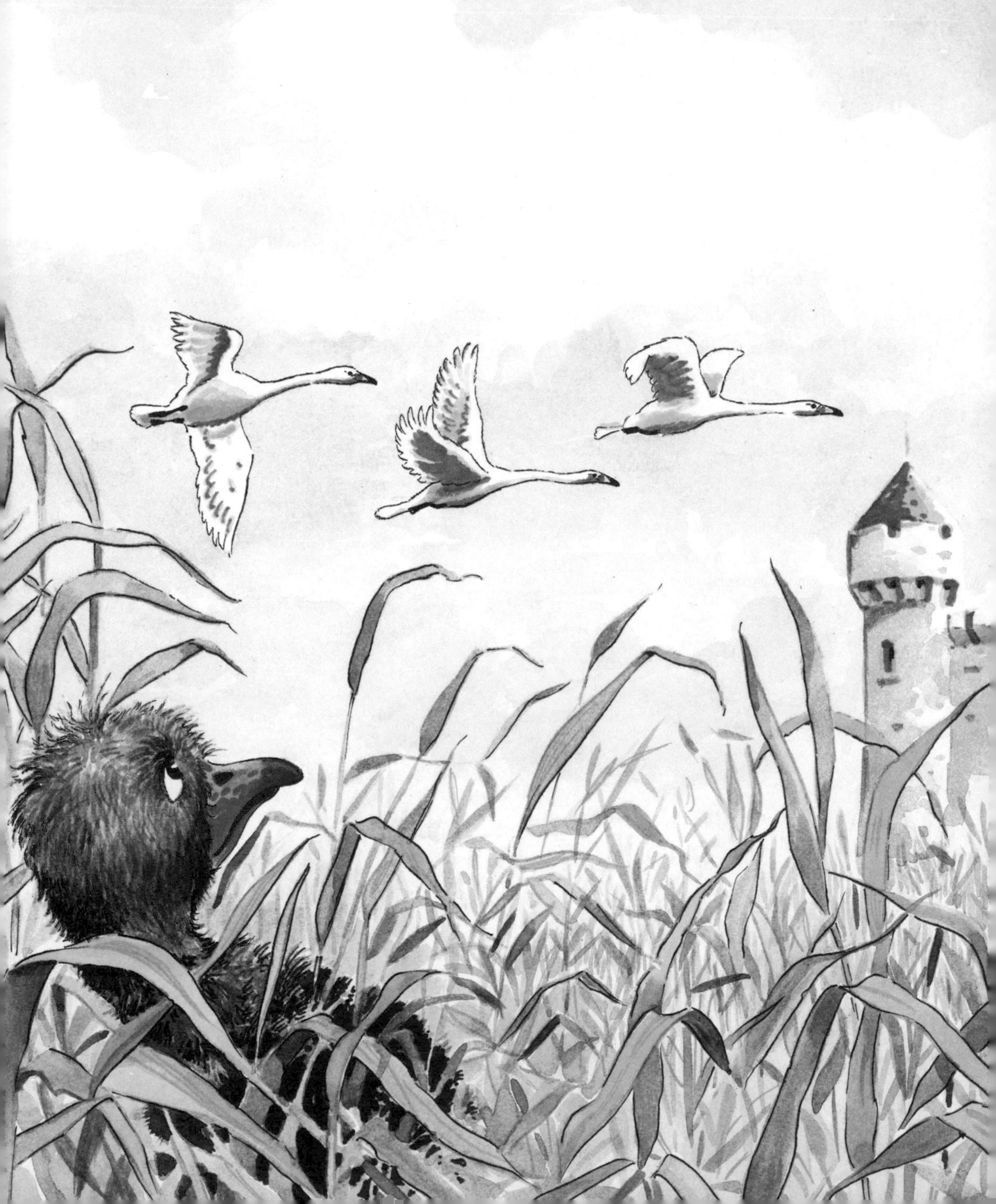

Soon, the flowers began to bloom and the days became warmer. It was spring again. To his surprise, the ugly duckling noticed that his wings had grown much larger than those of the other ducklings. One day he started to flap them. He rose out from the reeds and began to fly. He enjoyed the feeling of flying free through the air, and flew for a long time, until he came to a large lake. Looking down, he saw three lovely, white birds swimming in the water. They looked just like the ones he had seen flying overhead months before. The ugly duckling flew down to get a closer look. As he neared the surface of the lake, he saw a reflection of another of the lovely birds. The ugly duckling looked around, but there were no other birds in the sky.

Then he realised that he was looking at his own reflection in the water! He was the lovely bird flying so gracefully in the sky. He wasn't an ugly duckling after all. He was a beautiful, white swan.